Pick it up!

Written by Catherine Baker

Illustrated by Jon Stuart

Collins

Get a sun hat.

Get the rods and sacks.

3

Pick up the muck.

4

Pop it in the sack.

Pick up a rag.

Pop it in the sack.

Pick up a can.

Run and tip it in.

9

Get a red pen.

10

Pin it on the hut.

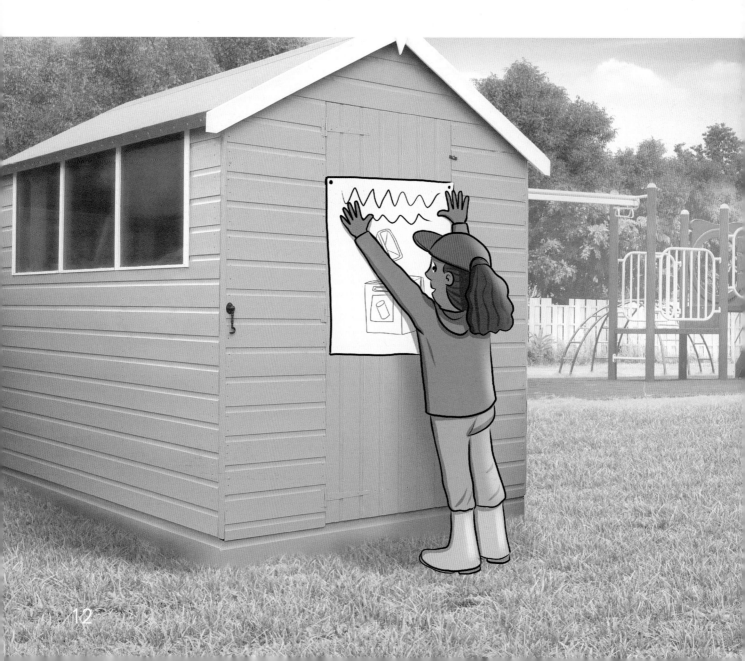

Get a hug!

/h/

14

After reading

Letters and Sounds: Phase 2

Word count: 54

Focus phonemes: /h/ /r/ /g/ /u/ /e/ /o/ /c/, ck

Common exception words: the, and

Curriculum links: Understanding the World: The world

Early learning goals: Reading: use phonic knowledge to decode regular words and read them aloud accurately; demonstrate understanding when talking with others about what they have read

Developing fluency

- Take turns to read with your child.
- Model reading the speech bubble on page 13 in different ways. Ask your child how they think it would be said in this book, for example in a grumpy voice, a happy voice, a whisper, shouted or frightened voice. (*happy/pleased/glad voice*)

Phonic practice

- Look together at words in the book that use the "c" grapheme (e.g. *can*) and words that use the "ck" grapheme (e.g. *pick*). Discuss how they make the same sound but are spelt differently, and challenge children to find other pages in the book that use them.
- Look at the "I spy sounds" pages together (14–15). Discuss what you can see. Ask your child: What items and actions can you find that begin with h and r? (e.g. *rackets, rug, robin, rainbow, raincoat, rocks, rake, rabbit, running, riding, railings, helicopter, hopscotch, hills, helmet, houses, handstands, headphones, hat*)

Extending vocabulary

- Look through the book together. Discuss the words that are used to describe the litter in the book. (*muck, can, pack, rag*)
- Explore other words to describe litter with your child. (e.g. *rubbish, trash, garbage, recycling or specific items such as plastic bottles, newspaper, crisp packets, drinks cans, wrappers, plastic bags, paper cups*)